Cockeyed

by William Missouri Downs

A SAMUEL FRENCH ACTING EDITION

FOUNDED 1830

NEW YORK HOLLYWOOD LONDON TORONTO

SAMUELFRENCH.COM

Copyright © 2007, 2009 by William Missouri Downs
Cover design by Steven Peck

ALL RIGHTS RESERVED

CAUTION: Professionals and amateurs are hereby warned that *COCK-EYED* is subject to a Licensing Fee. It is fully protected under the copyright laws of the United States of America, the British Commonwealth, including Canada, and all other countries of the Copyright Union. All rights, including professional, amateur, motion picture, recitation, lecturing, public reading, radio broadcasting, television and the rights of translation into foreign languages are strictly reserved. In its present form the play is dedicated to the reading public only.

The amateur live stage performance rights to *COCKEYED* are controlled exclusively by Samuel French, Inc., and licensing arrangements and performance licenses must be secured well in advance of presentation. PLEASE NOTE that amateur Licensing Fees are set upon application in accordance with your producing circumstances. When applying for a licensing quotation and a performance license please give us the number of performances intended, dates of production, your seating capacity and admission fee. Licensing Fees are payable one week before the opening performance of the play to Samuel French, Inc., at 45 W. 25th Street, New York, NY 10010.

Licensing Fee of the required amount must be paid whether the play is presented for charity or gain and whether or not admission is charged.

Stock licensing fees quoted upon application to Samuel French, Inc.

For all other rights than those stipulated above, apply to: Samuel French, Inc. 45 West 25th Street, New York, NY 10010.

Particular emphasis is laid on the question of amateur or professional readings, permission and terms for which must be secured in writing from Samuel French, Inc.

Copying from this book in whole or in part is strictly forbidden by law, and the right of performance is not transferable.

Whenever the play is produced the following notice must appear on all programs, printing and advertising for the play: "Produced by special arrangement with Samuel French, Inc."

Due authorship credit must be given on all programs, printing and advertising for the play.

ISBN 978-0-573-69716-6   Printed in U.S.A.   #29132

No one shall commit or authorize any act or omission by which the copyright of, or the right to copyright, this play may be impaired.

No one shall make any changes in this play for the purpose of production.

Publication of this play does not imply availability for performance. Both amateurs and professionals considering a production are strongly advised in their own interests to apply to Samuel French, Inc., for written permission before starting rehearsals, advertising, or booking a theatre.

No part of this book may be reproduced, stored in a retrieval system, or transmitted in any form, by any means, now known or yet to be invented, including mechanical, electronic, photocopying, recording, videotaping, or otherwise, without the prior written permission of the publisher.

IMPORTANT BILLING AND CREDIT
REQUIREMENTS

All producers of *COCKEYED* *must* give credit to the Author of the Play in all programs distributed in connection with performances of the Play, and in all instances in which the title of the Play appears for the purposes of advertising, publicizing or otherwise exploiting the Play and/ or a production. The name of the Author *must* appear on a separate line on which no other name appears, immediately following the title and *must* appear in size of type not less than fifty percent of the size of the title type.

COCKEYED was first produced by the HotCity Theatre in St. Louis. The production was directed by Marty Stanberry, with the following cast and crew:

PHIL . . . . Adam Flores
SOPHIA . . . . Jennifer Nitzband
NORMAN . . . . Paul Pagano
MARLEY . . . . Tyler Vickers

Scene Design – Alex Gaines
Lighting Design – Michael Sullivan
Costume Design – Felia Davenport
Sound Design – Jeff Griswold

COCKEYED's first workshop production was staged by the Cheyenne Little theatre. It was directed by Patti Kelly, with the following cast:

PHIL . . . . Brooks Reeves
SOPHIA . . . . Sarah Whittle
NORMAN . . . . Dale Williams
MARLEY . . . . Rory Mack

Special Thanks to: Lou Anne Wright, Harry Woods, Marty Stanberry, Jeff Tish, Dennis Madigan, Rich Burk, The Last Frontier Playwrights Conference, Chameleons Stage, Alex Gaines, Gwen Feldman, and Patti Kelly.

CAST OF CHARACTERS

PHIL – A Nice Guy (Majored in philosophy in college)
SOPHIA – A Pretty Secretary (She has a glass eye)
V.P. MARLEY – A Handsome Boss (He wears a Bluetooth ear cell phone)
NORMAN – A Nervous Accountant (Phil's friend)

SETTING

Setting: There are three small playing areas. At center is Sophia's tiny basement studio apartment. It has a kitchenette and a sleeper-sofa. She's been painting so the walls are mostly bare. On both sides of the studio set are areas that represent the offices of Hibarger Corporation.

On one side is Phil's pathetic office cubicle, on the other the stark employee break room – not much more than a table with a coffee machine.

TIME

The Present

PLACE

New York City

ACT ONE

*(Lights up on **PHIL** in his cluttered office cubicle.)*

PHIL. *(to the audience)* I've seen the woman I shall marry and she is without a doubt the most magnificent creature in all of New York – flawless except for one minor imperfection – she is totally unaware of my existence.

*(Lights up on **SOPHIA** in the break room.)*

PHIL. There, through yonder door, 'tis the company break room and – Sophia.

*(**SOPHIA** makes several cups of coffee. **PHIL** gazes upon her from his cubicle.)*

PHIL. *(to the audience)* I've often daydreamed what our life together would be like. One day we'd accidentally meet in the break room and instantaneously click. There'd be no kiss on the first date; no, we'd both be too excited about our five-hour dialogue on Plato's allegory of the cave as it relates to the movie *The Matrix.* The first kiss would come on our second date – after a six hour heart-to-heart on Hitler and existentialism, I'd take her in my arms and with total confidence – something I've never known – I'd kiss her. A soft sigh would escape from her, letting me know that she had never been kissed like that before.

*(During the following **NORMAN** enters and has a brief unheard conversation with **SOPHIA**.)*

PHIL. *(to the audience)* On our wedding night we'd make love like Sartre and Simone de Beauvoir – And it would never get old. After which we'd lie in each other's arms and watch PBS or Book TV, or some other intellectually stimulating program.

*(**NORMAN** exits.)*

PHIL. *(to the audience)* Kids? Lots. Marcus, René, Immanuel and the twins Jean-Paul and Ayn – twins run in her family – all straight "A" students – except for Ayn, she's having trouble with Sartre's *Essay on Phenomenological Ontology* – but that's okay, she's only in the third grade.

(V.P. MARLEY enters and talks to SOPHIA. He wears a hands-free Bluetooth cell phone piece imbedded in his ear. We do not hear their short conversation.)

PHIL. *(to the audience)* Then would come graduation day – Marcus, summa cum laude from Yale, René summa cum laude from Harvard, Immanuel, University of Michigan class valedictorian and the twins, Jean-Paul and Ayn, both Rhodes Scholars – We sure missed them when they were in England, but they flew home every weekend to do laundry. And all of them philosophy majors – just like their father – only, unlike their father, they find good paying jobs with full benefits.

(V.P. MARLEY exits. SOPHIA is finally alone for a moment. She sips her green tea; it's been a hard day.)

PHIL. *(to the audience)* And then one night, after a long evening with the family and extended family, I'd turn to Sophia and say "I think I'm a little tired." And we'd go upstairs. And make passionate love even though we're well into our nineties. After which, I'd lie in her arms. She'd play with my hair. And the last words I'd hear would be "I love you sweetheart" as I drift off into a higher dimension, or non-existence, or whatever transcendental thing you wish to insert here. Aristotle says at the beginning of *Metaphysics*, "We take delight in our senses – apart from their usefulness they are loved for their own sake and none more than the sense of sight." I am in love with the sight of Sophia.

NORMAN. *(Offstage)* Phil! Phil!

(NORMAN rushes in.)

NORMAN. *(in a panic)* Phil! Problem! The Mead Report. These figures aren't adding up.

PHIL. *(not taking his eyes off SOPHIA)* The Mead report. It's right here.

(PHIL hands his wallet to NORMAN.)

NORMAN. This is your wallet!

PHIL. *(not paying attention)* I think you'll find the figures balance out nicely.

NORMAN. We need to talk –.

PHIL. Wait! She's scratching her nostril! Wow!

NORMAN. Phil, we got problems –.

PHIL. Sometimes when she makes coffee she seems to look over at me. I think she likes what she sees.

NORMAN. Who's this?

PHIL. Sophia.

NORMAN. Sophia? That's not possible.

PHIL. Why not?

NORMAN. She's a beautiful woman. You're a nice guy.

PHIL. So what?

NORMAN. Beautiful women aren't interested in nice guys.

PHIL. Says who?

NORMAN. Ask any beautiful woman. They want a guy who has sophistication, a guy with breeding, a guy with a Porsche. "Nice" isn't part of the equation.

PHIL. That's the difference between you and me, Norm. You accept what life hands you. You're nothing but a wallflower; I'm what Nietzsche called a superman.

NORMAN. Phil, you're falling behind. I've been covering for you, buddy, but I can't do it much longer –.

(SOPHIA exits.)

PHIL. Wait! She's walking. What a great walk. And. She's. Gone. Wow, she was in the break room for almost five minutes. I'm all tingly – !

NORMAN. Phil. Try to concentrate. Look at me. Over here. *(grabbing PHIL's head)* Vice President Marley is on the warpath – ! And if this merger goes through you know there'll be layoffs. Did you hear me?

PHIL. Yes.

NORMAN. What did I say?

PHIL. She's wearing blue today.

NORMAN. Phil, I didn't want to say this but you've given me no choice. This isn't easy. Phil – you're average. Not that average is bad. Most of us are average – I'm average! Sophia is what we average call *above average*. Am I making myself clear – ?

(SOPHIA enters and makes more coffee.)

PHIL. *(He hauls out opera glasses to watch her.)* She's back! Seven coffee trips in one morning! A new record!

NORMAN. Phil, listen to me kid, you haven't got a chance!

PHIL. *(watching SOPHIA)* I love how she stirs.

NORMAN. That's it. You're talking to her.

PHIL. What? Now?

NORMAN. Yes, now.

PHIL. But I'm late with the Mead report.

NORMAN. Just 'cause we've been friends since childhood and I hired you when absolutely no one would hire a philosophy major, is no reason to assume that I will not fire you right now!

PHIL. What would I say?

NORMAN. What does it matter? I just need you to say "hello" so that she can reject you, so you can fall into a lovesick depression, swear off women, and get back to work. Look, I chat with her every day. She's an okay person – perhaps a little self-absorbed, but approachable. So do it.

PHIL. Do what?

NORMAN. Say "hello" to her.

PHIL. I can't.

NORMAN. Why not?

PHIL. I'm too nice.

NORMAN. Go make coffee.

PHIL. What?

NORMAN. You're my assistant – make me coffee.

PHIL. That's not in my job description –.

NORMAN. If there isn't coffee on my desk in two minutes, you're fired.

PHIL. Okay. Okay. I'm going to do it. I'm going to say "hello" to the most beautiful woman in Manhattan. And then, I'm going to marry her –

NORMAN. One step at a time. She's resting. Now's your chance.

*(**PHIL.** hits his mouth with a heavy dose of breath spray.)*

PHIL. *(to himself)* Okay, calm. Keep calm…I am a rock. I have an island. A calm rock.

*(**PHIL.** nonchalantly approaches **SOPHIA**. She stirs her tea – off in her own little world. **PHIL.** acts as though he's looking for something. Finally, he speaks.)*

PHIL. Hi.

(She doesn't respond.)

PHIL. *(nervous)* It's Phil from accounting…*(no response)* Isn't that something, I also prefer green tea with Sweet and Low…*(awkward beat)* Great name…I mean I love it when a product says what it is – It's sweet and yet it's also low…like…Animal Crackers, it's all there in the name.

*(**SOPHIA** sips her hot tea not paying the slightest attention to him. **PHIL.** looks to **NORMAN** for support. **NORMAN** waves him on.)*

PHIL. Did I mention that I'm from accounting? Yes, I'm an accountant. That's right. Matter of fact I'm head of accounting…Yep, that's my…wing…

*(Nothing from **SOPHIA**, she simply sips her tea.)*

PHIL. …Okay you got me. I'm not an accountant; I'm an accountant's assistant. I was a philosophy major in college – I know women find that a big turn off. I once told a blind date I majored in philosophy – she changed her identity so I wouldn't call her anymore. At least I didn't major in English – she probably would've faked her own death.

(Still nothing from her.)

PHIL. So…what are your thoughts on Hitler and existentialism?

(SOPHIA *lets out a little sigh and exits.)*

PHIL. Well, nice talking to you – Same time tomorrow?

(PHIL *runs back over to* **NORMAN**.*)*

NORMAN. How did it go?

PHIL. What was I thinking? If I've told you once I've told you a million times, Norm, never try to talk to women. It's always better to admire them from a distance – tomorrow I'm breaking it off with her.

NORMAN. What did I tell you –.

PHIL. I've been rejected before but never like this. On rare occasions I've met women who were less than impressed. You know the type, you say "hello" and the way she says "hello" back lets you know that you're a lifeless schmuck who hasn't got a chance. Women must take classes from Lee Strasberg to get all of that subtext into a simple "hello." But this…this…secretary – won't even look at me.

NORMAN. I told you, she's a little self-absorbed.

PHIL. Self-absorbed? She looked straight through me!

NORMAN. Phil, I didn't want to say this but the rumor around the office is that she has –

PHIL. Oh God, not herpes again.

NORMAN. No…she has a glass eye.

PHIL. A what?

NORMAN. A glass eye. A fake eye.

PHIL. You gotta be kidding. Which?

NORMAN. The receptionist thinks it's the right.

PHIL. How do you know?

NORMAN. Some chump in human resources was teasing her about it.

PHIL. Oh my God! That explains everything. I was standing to her right! She never saw me. Wow, for a microsecond I thought I was a loser.

(**SOPHIA** *steps up to the coffee station and makes another round of coffee.*)

NORMAN. She's back.

PHIL. And she has a glass eye. Isn't that wonderful!

(**SOPHIA** *accidentally knocks over a cup of coffee.*)

SOPHIA. Oh no.

(*She grabs for the paper towels but has no depth perception.*)

PHIL. It's a sign! This is the *in* I was hoping for. You gotta introduce me. That's how most office romances start, with an innocent introduction in the break room. But don't tell her I'm your assistant. Tell her I'm – a consultant. Wait, executive consultant!

NORMAN. If I do this will you go back to work?

PHIL. You do this and I'm all over the Mead report.

NORMAN. Her back's turned, let's go.

PHIL. No, not so fast. We need a plan. How about if we just happen to be passing and then you say, "Oh, Sophia, let me introduce you to Phil, my boss."

NORMAN. But I'm your boss.

PHIL. Okay, we'll compromise, senior executive consultant. And I'll say, "Oh, it's nice to meet you." And you'll say something like, "You two have lots of commonalities." What do we have in common?

NORMAN. Not philosophy.

PHIL. How do you know, she might be a Kierkegaard Groupie – Wait! That's right – I read in "It's All My Fault" – the existentialist newsletter – there's a Mensa square dance at the Armory next weekend. We could double date.

NORMAN. Whatever you do, don't invite her to dance.

PHIL. Why not?

NORMAN. Cause you can't dance.

PHIL. Can't dance. Can't dance! I'll have you know I took first place in the disco dance-off at the last Philosopher's Ball.

NORMAN. There are so many things wrong with that state-
ment I don't know where to begin.

(**NORMAN** *starts towards* **SOPHIA**.)

PHIL. Wait wait wait.

(**PHIL** *again hits his mouth with breath spray. He sprays
his armpits and crotch too.*)

(**NORMAN** *crosses to* **SOPHIA**.)

NORMAN. Hi, Sophia.

SOPHIA. Hey, Norm.

NORMAN. Need a hand?

SOPHIA. Oh thanks.

(**NORMAN** *helps* **SOPHIA** *clean up the mess.*)

(**PHIL** *walks up.*)

PHIL. *(unnatural – making up a topic)* …Oh hello, Norm. I
just thought I'd get some green tea. There it is.

SOPHIA. *(to* **NORMAN***)* We're out of paper towels.

NORMAN. I'll have my *assistant* get some. You okay?

SOPHIA. I'm fine…No, I'm not. I'm having a horrible day.
Four years at Vassar and what do I do? Get coffee.

PHIL. *(whispering to* **NORMAN***)* Left, I have to be on the left.

SOPHIA. Everyone says it's a mistake dating your boss but
did I listen?

NORMAN. You're dating Vice President Marley?

SOPHIA. Yeah. And he's the same at lunch. I ordered lunch
in yesterday. I thought, you know, maybe we could be
alone for a moment. What does he do? You guessed it,
"Sweetheart, be a darling and get me some decaf."

PHIL. I hate coffee. It makes me diuretic.

SOPHIA. I promised myself that I'd never get involved with
anyone at work.

PHIL. I'm thinking of quitting.

SOPHIA. And get this; he dropped *the hint* the other day.
The "M" word. He was talking about the pending possible merger with Mead Corporation and he compared

it to "a marriage." And he emphasized "marriage" and met my gaze for a moment. Then this morning I saw a huge diamond ring in his desk drawer.

NORMAN. Wow, he's serious.

SOPHIA. But I'm not so sure. He's been married twice before. But he does have a corner office and a Porsche.

NORMAN. *(throwing this to NORMAN)* A Porsche, imagine that.

SOPHIA. Mother says all I date are losers.

PHIL. I have a mother.

SOPHIA. "You can fall in love with a rich man just as easily as a poor one." I suppose she's right. I mean money is important, but I can't help but think that I'm just being shallow. God, I wish I could meet the right man.

(PHIL clears his throat.)

NORMAN. Oh, Sophia, I want you to meet Phil, my assistant –

PHIL. Senior executive management assistant.

NORMAN. I think you might have a lot in common.

SOPHIA. *(not paying attention)* Oh, did I tell you? Mom found me an apartment –

NORMAN. We were childhood friends –

SOPHIA. A horrible basement studio with no windows. It's a cave, but at least I can afford it.

NORMAN. We went to college together.

SOPHIA. Excuse me?

NORMAN. Phil and I.

SOPHIA. Who?

NORMAN. Phil. My assistant.

PHIL. Senior executive assistant in charge of accounting. That's my wing.

(SOPHIA turns and looks right through PHIL.)

SOPHIA. What's going on?

NORMAN. Nothing, I just thought you two should meet.

PHIL. Because we have tons of commonalities.

(*PHIL offers his hand.* SOPHIA *stares blankly through him.*)

SOPHIA. ...Is this a joke?

NORMAN. No, I just –.

SOPHIA. What do you want me to meet? Dead air? The coffee machine?

NORMAN. No, I just thought you and Phil should –.

SOPHIA. Who's Phil?

NORMAN. The person standing beside me.

SOPHIA. Norm, this isn't funny.

PHIL. Are you sure it's the right; maybe it's the left?

SOPHIA. I spill my heart out and what do you do, introduce me to a coffee machine. Ha ha – very funny.

NORMAN. Sophia, wait, it's no joke. I really want you to meet Phil.

(SOPHIA *sees nothing.*)

SOPHIA. Everyone in this office is a sicko. I expect that from the jerk in human resources but not from you, Norm.

(SOPHIA *exits. Beat.*)

NORMAN. What just happened?

PHIL. I told you – she acts as if I don't exist!

NORMAN. What've you done? You've been gawking at her with your stupid opera glasses haven't you! Great, I've introduced my boss's secretary to the office pervert. I've never been so humiliated.

(PHIL *follows* NORMAN *back over to the cubicle.*)

PHIL. You're humiliated? She thought I was a coffee machine!

NORMAN. Phil, these are the last words on the subject. Are you listening? Women like that aren't interested in nice guys. You haven't got a chance.

PHIL. She's a self-absorbed paper-pusher with a glass eye! If I can't make it with her then who the hell can I make it with?!

NORMAN. Marybeth in accounts receivable.

PHIL. Who?

NORMAN. Marybeth – the girl with the crutches. I introduced you to her last week.

PHIL. I talked to someone on crutches?

NORMAN. You met her at the office Christmas party.

PHIL. Norm, if I talked to someone on crutches I'd've remembered.

NORMAN. We talked about her physical therapy and how after it's over she'll have only a slight limp. You talked for, like, fifteen minutes – the shy girl with the southern accent.

PHIL. I have no memory of her.

NORMAN. I can set you up.

PHIL. You want to set me up with a shy southern girl with a limp?

NORMAN. She just broke up with her physical therapist. She told me she thought you were nice.

PHIL. Great, you've got me a date with Laura from *The Glass Menagerie* – Whoopee!

NORMAN. Phil, you're always biting off more than you can chew – remember when you asked Michelle Oxford to go to the senior prom?

PHIL. She was bulimic and had a low opinion of herself – I thought I had a chance.

NORMAN. She was homecoming queen, head cheerleader, class president and a lesbian –.

PHIL. And bulimic with a low opinion of herself –

NORMAN. When she refused what did you do?

PHIL. *(a little ashamed)* ...I followed her home.

NORMAN. You followed her to college! You became a women's studies minor so you could follow her around campus. Phil, this has gotta stop. No means no, and a restraining order means never. But in this case it's even worse. Sophia obviously thinks so little of you that you don't even exist.

PHIL. Fine, it's over. Now if you'll excuse me.

NORMAN. Phil, you're going to find the right person. I swear, someday it'll happen. Now go through whatever depressive stuff you need to go through in order to justify this complete humiliation and get back to work.

(NORMAN exits.)

PHIL. *(to the audience)* I know what you're thinking. The philosopher Descartes, right? Of course you are. In *Discourse on the Method,* 1637, Descartes wrote "Cogito ergo sum." "I think therefore I exist." But what good is existence if people look right through you? Perhaps the stoic philosophers were right – once you reconcile yourself to the imperfectability of life you become less bitter, less prone to self-pity and more likely to date repressed Tennessee William's characters.

(NORMAN enters.)

NORMAN. Are you happy with yourself? I just saw Sophia leave. Apparently she was so upset by what you did she went home.

PHIL. What did I do?

(V.P. MARLEY enters with a file. He has a hands-free Bluetooth cell phone receiver embedded in his ear.)

V.P. MARLEY. What's going on here?

NORMAN. Vice President Marley!

V.P. MARLEY. Who are you?

NORMAN. Me sir? I'm an accountant. I'm working on the Mead report.

V.P. MARLEY. How's it coming?

NORMAN. Practically almost done, sir. Phil and I are on top of it.

V.P. MARLEY. Phil? Who's Phil?

NORMAN. My assistant.

V.P. MARLEY. Never heard of him –

(He places a finger on his Bluetooth.)

V.P. MARLEY. *(into his ear cell phone receiver)* Hello?…No. Cancel my tennis lesson, get me some coffee and bring my Porsche around. By the way, have you been in my office?…Well?

NORMAN. Oh, you're talking to me. Of course not, I'd never go near your office, sir.

V.P. MARLEY. It must've been Sophia then. She went home. Apparently some jerk introduced her to a coffee machine as a practical joke.

NORMAN. Who would do such a thing?

V.P. MARLEY. Don't know but if I find out he's fired.

NORMAN. Couldn't agree more, sir.

V.P. MARLEY. *(into his earpiece)* No!

NORMAN. No?

V.P. MARLEY. *(into his earpiece)* …No, I said cancel the tennis lesson. *(to **NORMAN**)* She must've accidentally taken the wrong file off my desk. So, call a messenger, have him take this file to her apartment and bring back the one she took by mistake, okay?…Okay?!

NORMAN. *(still confused as to whom **MARLEY** is addressing)* Oh! Me. Right. I'll do it right away.

*(**V.P. MARLEY** hands **NORMAN** a file and a piece of paper with an address on it.)*

NORMAN. *(to **PHIL**)* Get a messenger up here right away.

*(**PHIL** dials.)*

V.P. MARLEY. I've also looked over the preliminary report concerning the merger.

NORMAN. I thought you'd be pleased sir.

V.P. MARLEY. It's crap.

NORMAN. That's what I meant.

V.P. MARLEY. Matter of fact this is the crappiest report I've ever read.

NORMAN. I couldn't agree more, sir.

PHIL. *(on phone)* We need a messenger on the tenth floor. When?

NORMAN. Now!

PHIL. *(on phone)* Now!

(PHIL hangs up.)

V.P. MARLEY. And to top it off there's a love letter addressed to the "Miss Sweet and Low Lady" signed, "You know who" stuck inside. I think someone's forgot my regulation concerning office romances.

NORMAN. I'll send out an office wide e-mail immediately reminding everyone of your policy.

V.P. MARLEY. What's our company motto?

NORMAN. "Accountability and rock-solid ethical standards give us our competitive edge."

V.P. MARLEY. Whatever you do never ever forget that...ah... ah...

NORMAN. Norman, sir.

V.P. MARLEY. Now make these numbers work. Feel free to work all night if you have to. Final report on my desk noon tomorrow. And if you find out who this practical joker is let me know.

NORMAN. I'm on top of it, sir.

V.P. MARLEY. *(into his earpiece)* No, I said cancel my tennis lesson...And bring me some coffee!

(V.P. MARLEY exits.)

NORMAN. *(calling after)* No slip-ups. Noon on the nose, sir, no later!

(NORMAN waits for V.P. MARLEY to get out of sight and whacks PHIL.)

NORMAN. See what you did! I'm on his radar now!

PHIL. Radar?

NORMAN. Rule one when working in an office – stay under the radar. Gotta do damage control. Get on the report. Make the numbers work, I don't care how – just do it. And one more screw up, one slight infraction, if you so much as look at a female in this office, you'll be where all philosophy majors are.

PHIL. Searching for truth?

NORMAN. Unemployed!

(NORMAN runs out.)

PHIL. *(to the audience)* I know what you're thinking, where is Kierkegaard when you need him? Am I right?... Kierkegaard...The Danish philosopher. 1813 – 1855. Before Sartre, Kierkegaard said that we have choices – That the most fundamental choice is between existence and non-existence. That the moment we make a choice is the moment we begin to exist.

(PHIL picks up the sheet of paper with SOPHIA's address.)

PHIL. 69 West 77th Street, lower level, apartment B. *(to the audience)* I know, don't do it. It'll only end in disaster. I'll get fired. My heart'll be broken. I'll lose my best friend. But, unlike you, who are passively sitting in the dark doing nothing, I choose to exist.

(He dials his phone.)

PHIL. *(on phone)* It's Phil –....Phil in accounting. Cancel the messenger.

(PHIL hangs up.)

PHIL. *(to the audience)* It's time that the nice guys of the world let the above average looking women of the world know that we exist! Cogito ergo Zoom!

(He sprays his breath, underarms, and then grabs the address and envelope and exits.)

(Lights up on SOPHIA's one room basement apartment. She enters – It hasn't been a good day. She blows her nose and sighs. The phone rings.)

SOPHIA. *(on phone)* Hi Mom...How did I know it was you? It's always you...Let me take off my coat and I'll call you back...No he didn't propose today...Mom, I just walked in, I'm cold and tired and...something stinks.... Yes. I took out the trash...Because I always take out the trash before I leave in the morning...Look, Mom, I'll call you back in five...Yes, promise.

(She grabs a bag of trash from under the sink and opens the front door. There stands **PHIL** *with the file and a gorgeous bouquet of flowers. He jumps.)*

PHIL. Oh hi! It's Phil from accounting. Sorry, didn't mean to startle me – I mean, you – I mean, you startled me.

(Totally ignoring him, **SOPHIA** *walks right by him and drops the trash in a garbage can in the hallway.)*

PHIL. We met in the break room today...flowers? They're for me – I mean for me from you.

*(***SOPHIA*** *walks back in and slams the door in his face.)*

PHIL. *(calling through the door)* Did anyone ever tell you that you're not a nice person?! As a matter of fact you may be one of the biggest bitc – Not nice person's I've ever met!

*(***SOPHIA*** *realizes that she forgot an empty bottle. She grabs it and heads back to the door.)*

PHIL. *(calling through the door)* Everyone in the office says that you're a self important, self-centered, self-absorbed and – !

*(***SOPHIA*** *opens the door. They are face to face.)*

PHIL. *(suddenly sweet)* Hi! It's Phil from accounting. We met in the break room today. You might've accidentally taken the wrong file off Mr. Marley's desk –.

(While he is talking **SOPHIA** *again walks right by him, dumps the bottle in the garbage, walks back into her apartment, and slams the door in his face.)*

PHIL. *(screaming through the door)* You're not a human being!

(During the following **SOPHIA** *sits on the foldout couch and begins to cry.)*

PHIL. *(screaming through the door)* You're a monster! A horrible narcissistic she-devil with a glass eye! And here are your flowers. I am destroying your flowers! *(muffled sounds as* **PHIL** *struggles to obliterate the bouquet)* There! And just so you know, you haven't done any damage to

my self-respect! I may never date again, not even Marybeth the quiet girl with the slight limp in accounts
receivable, but my self-respect is intact! Do you hear
me, totally intact!

(**SOPHIA** *gently cries. Beat.*)

PHIL. *(talking through the door)* Sophia? *(no response)* Are you
crying? *(no response)* Hey, look maybe we didn't get off
on the right foot. You know, what you did in the break
room today wasn't, you gotta admit, very nice. *(still no
response.)* Sophia? I'm coming in…

(**PHIL** *nudges open the door. He holds the file and a
totally annihilated bouquet of flowers. There are even
twisted bits of flower remnants on his coat left over from
his vicious attack. He finds* **SOPHIA** *sitting on the couch
quietly sniffling.*)

PHIL. Your flowers. Ah…They were damaged in transit.

(The phone rings. **SOPHIA** *answers.)*

SOPHIA. *(on phone)* Mom, it hasn't been five minutes. …No
it's been three minutes. I'll call in two minutes.

(**SOPHIA** *hangs up. Upset, she buries her head in her
hands.* **PHIL** *slowly enters and sits down beside her on
the foldout couch.)*

PHIL. Look, I know life is tough. Relationships are difficult.
But you don't want Vice President Marley. He's been
married before. Both nasty divorces – rumor is, one
ended in a duel. Sophia, I know I'm not in your league
but if you'll just give me a chance. Or even, maybe, a
fleeting glance…Sophia? Hello…Earth to Sophia…

*(He waves his hand in front of her face. She blows her
nose.)*

PHIL. Helloooo. It's Phil from accounting…Sophia? *(nothing from her)* Okay, this is kinda freaky.

*(Beat. He sticks his thumbs in his ears and wiggles his
hands)*

PHIL. *(singsong)* La La La La La La!

(Still nothing. He thinks for a moment. Then shoots her the bird.)

PHIL. I'm shooting you the bird. Right in your face. … You really can't see me can you? But I exist. Descartes said, I think therefore I exist. So I exist…because I am thinking…or am I just thinking that I'm thinking. Sophia, I beg you to tell me that you can hear and see me – Wait – if you can't see me, can you see this!?

(He picks up a pen off the coffee table and holds it in front of her face.)

PHIL. I'm floating. I'm a pen and I'm floating. *(She sees nothing.)* Nothing. I don't exist and so nothing I touch exists.

(SOPHIA lets out a little sigh.)

SOPHIA. *(to herself)* Oh well, another evening alone.

(She exits to the bathroom.)

PHIL. *(to the audience)* I know what you're thinking. First, when Descartes said, "I think therefore I exist" he only claimed his own existence — he didn't prove the existence of others. Secondly, it's important to remember that I'm really really freaked out right now! Okay, okay calm down. Something's happened. Perhaps I've entered some kind of hyperspace or dualistic reality. Or maybe there's only one reality, but two ways of perceiving it. I mean, there are colors we can't perceive and sounds we can't hear so why can't there be people we can't see? Take Marybeth in receiving – Norm claims I had a fifteen-minute conversation with her, yet I remember none of it, so technically does she exist?

(SOPHIA steps from the bathroom. She wears an eye patch and holds her glass eye – PHIL is amazed. She puts the glass eye in a special box and then she reaches into her bra and pulls out falsies – PHIL is even more amazed. The phone rings.)

SOPHIA. *(on phone)* …Yes Mom. I'm fine… I just needed

to take my eye out and get comfortable...what?... No, I've never told him about my eye. ...Yes, I know that's a real turn off to men.

PHIL. I don't find it a turn off at all.

SOPHIA. *(on phone)* No, I left work early...didn't feel well.

PHIL. *(inspecting the glass eye)* Wow.

SOPHIA. *(on phone)* ...Oh nothing. This guy in accounting, who's usually really nice, played a stupid practical joke on me. He introduced me to a coffee machine. I know everyone thinks I'm a real loser, but that was just out of bounds...

PHIL. You? A loser? My god Sophia, don't you realize you're every nice guy's dream?

SOPHIA. *(on phone)* ...Mr. Marley? I like him but I'm not sure...Yes, he makes a lot of money. But when I kiss him I don't feel much. It's like his lips don't exist... Mom, I gotta find someone who would like me for me – eye patch and all.

PHIL. Sophia, when I was a kid, I was really turned on by the girl on the Bacardi rum bottle.

SOPHIA. *(on phone)* Someone who doesn't try to make a move on the first date.

PHIL. I know what you mean; it's always so awkward. It should come naturally and not be...and not be... what's the word I'm looking for?

SOPHIA. *(on phone)* Forced.

PHIL. Exactly!

SOPHIA. *(on phone)* Kids?

PHIL. Lots?

SOPHIA. *(on phone)* Two or three would be nice. But most importantly someone who will treat me with respect.

PHIL. My god, Sophia, that's me! Besides breaking into your apartment and flipping you off, I've always treated you with respect.

SOPHIA. *(on phone)* Yes Mom, I know the rules...okay. One more time. The way to catch a man. One – never admit that I have a glass eye. Two – never admit I think the best band in all of Rock & Roll history was the Bee Gees. And above all never ever tell him I was a philosophy major in college.

PHIL. Oh, my, god!

SOPHIA. *(on phone)* Mom, it's tough having you living right upstairs from me – Sometimes I feel like you're listening in – wait a minute, Mom, got another call. *(She pushes the flash button.)* Hello…Oh hi…Where are you?…You're kidding. …Oh, not a problem come on down. *(She pushes the flash button.)* Mom, it's him! Who? Him! Vice President Marley!

PHIL. Here?

SOPHIA. Yes, he's here!…Mom, I gotta go. Bye.

*(**SOPHIA** runs for the bathroom.)*

PHIL. Eye eye eye!

SOPHIA. Oh, right!

*(She grabs the glass eye and runs into the bathroom. **PHIL** heads for the door.)*

PHIL. Sophia. Look, I know you can't see or hear me but I just want to say it's been real. See you at work tomorrow – well you won't *see* me but I'll *see* you.

*(**PHIL** starts to exit but just as he gets to the door **V.P. MARLEY** knocks.)*

PHIL. Oh crap.

(Panicked, he looks for a place to hide.)

V.P. MARLEY. *(calling through the door)* Sophia?

SOPHIA. *(Offstage)* Coming!

*(**PHIL** runs into the kitchenette and hides just as the door opens.)*

V.P. MARLEY. Your door's open. I'm just going to let myself in.

SOPHIA. *(from the bathroom)* I'll be right out!

*(**V.P. MARLEY** gets a call)*

V.P. MARLEY. *(responding to earpiece)* Hello! No. I said sell

Amalgamated. Buy Mead…That's right…Yes, I'll hold.

(V.P. MARLEY looks around the place.)

V.P. MARLEY. Sweetheart?

SOPHIA. *(from the bathroom)* Yes!

V.P. MARLEY. Did a messenger stop by?

SOPHIA. *(from the bathroom)* A messenger? No.

V.P. MARLEY. You didn't happen to take a file off my desk by any chance?

SOPHIA. *(from the bathroom)* A what?

V.P. MARLEY. There was this file containing some V.I.P. stuff on my desk and suddenly it's missing. *(responding to earpiece)* Yes. I'm still holding.

(SOPHIA enters sans eyepatch.)

SOPHIA. Hi.

V.P. MARLEY. Your door was open so I…

SOPHIA. No problem.

V.P. MARLEY. You look…great.

SOPHIA. *(nonchalantly adjusting her eye)* Thanks.

(They kiss.)

V.P. MARLEY. Fetch me a cup of coffee will ya?

SOPHIA. Decaf?

V.P. MARLEY. You read my mind.

(SOPHIA goes to the kitchenette. In hiding, PHIL has a nice view of her legs. She's still trying to get her eye seated. V.P. MARLEY looks around the place.)

V.P. MARLEY. So, this is your new place.

SOPHIA. Yeah. It'll have to be instant.

V.P. MARLEY. You need more pictures.

SOPHIA. Oh, I've been painting. Can't decide on a color.

V.P. MARLEY. Feels like a cave.

SOPHIA. I know but I think I can make it work.

(She accidentally knocks over a coffee cup, spilling its hot contents on the invisible PHIL's crotch.)

SOPHIA. Oh no.

V.P. MARLEY. Problem?

SOPHIA. Just a little mess, got it.

> *(She grabs a paper towel and cleans. During the follow-*
> *ing this cleaning includes reaching down right between*
> **PHIL**'s *legs – near his crotch.* **PHIL** *is both shocked and*
> *thrilled.)*

V.P. MARLEY. Look, Sweetheart, you left the office awfully
sudden.

SOPHIA. Yes. I wasn't feeling well.

V.P. MARLEY. I heard there was an event in the break room.

SOPHIA. Oh, that. It was nothing – A practical joke that's
all.

V.P. MARLEY. You know I have regulations prohibiting practical jokes.

SOPHIA. It wasn't that big a deal.

V.P. MARLEY. Sophia, I'm a little concerned. When you left
the office I thought perhaps there was something else
wrong.

SOPHIA. *(nonchalantly trying to get her eye to seat)* Wrong?
What could be wrong?

V.P. MARLEY. I know it must be awkward dating your boss.
But from the moment you walked in my office, I knew
you were something special. You had a sparkle that
most worker bees lack.

SOPHIA. Worker bees?

V.P. MARLEY. That's just a term management uses. I just
couldn't see someone as pretty as you standing in
unemployment lines just because you made a mistake
in college.

SOPHIA. Mistake?

V.P. MARLEY. Majoring in philosophy.

SOPHIA. Oh. Right. That mistake.

V.P. MARLEY. As you know Hibarger Corporation, like most
companies, have rules prohibiting the hiring of philosophy majors, but I skirted them.

SOPHIA. And I'm grateful.

V.P. MARLEY. I guess what I'm trying to say is, I think it's important that we be honest.

SOPHIA. I agree.

V.P. MARLEY. So, if you took a file off my desk, even by mistake, you'd tell me.

SOPHIA. Of course.

V.P. MARLEY. So what did you do with it?

SOPHIA. With what?

V.P. MARLEY. The file.

SOPHIA. It wasn't me.

V.P. MARLEY. Sophia, honey, you're the only person who went in my office.

SOPHIA. I swear it wasn't me. ·

V.P. MARLEY. *(responding to earpiece)* That's bull!

SOPHIA. Excuse me.

V.P. MARLEY. *(responding to earpiece)* That's bull! Don't tell me you can't buy Mead…Yes, I'll hold. *(to* **SOPHIA***)* Sorry business.

SOPHIA. Of course. I understand.

V.P. MARLEY. Come. Sit.

(He sits on the foldout couch.)

SOPHIA. Sure.

(She joins him.)

V.P. MARLEY. Just want to say I've never met anyone like you. I know we haven't been dating for a long time but they've been good dates. And except for that time you launched into that twenty-minute diatribe about Hitler and existentialism we clicked. And as you know I'm a take action sorta guy. That's why I'm where I am and who I am. That's why I earn well over a million a year. Plus perks. Lots of perks – like the condo in Cancun and the corporate getaway in Barbados.

(The phone rings.)

SOPHIA. *(on the phone)* Yes, Mom? *(She turns away so he can't quite hear.)* …Yes, it's in and adjusted. Goodbye.

(She hangs up.)

V.P. MARLEY. What's "in?"

SOPHIA. Excuse me?

V.P. MARLEY. You said it's "in" and "adjusted."

SOPHIA. Oh, that. I'm…I'm cooking a turkey for Mother. It's *in* the oven and the oven is *adjusted.*

V.P. MARLEY. You know, sweetheart, when two companies… amalgamate they really need to get to know each other. You know, check each other out. And as you know, next week my divorce is final. So I was thinking that maybe you and I could perhaps enter into a formal agreement. You know, share stock options.

(The phone rings. **SOPHIA** *picks up the receiver and hangs up.)*

SOPHIA. Look, Richard –.

V.P. MARLEY. Want me to say it, okay; I'm in love with you.

SOPHIA. And I have strong feelings for you –.

V.P. MARLEY. I'll prove it.

SOPHIA. Prove what?

V.P. MARLEY. I'll prove how I feel.

(He gets down on one knee.)

V.P. MARLEY. Sophia, sweetheart, what I'm trying to say is… *(responding to earpiece)* Shut up!

SOPHIA. Excuse me?

V.P. MARLEY. *(responding to earpiece)* Shut up! He didn't… Okay we gotta do an end run. Call Frankie in the London office and let him know what's going on… Can't talk right now, I'm proposing. I'll call you back in a minute.

(He hangs up.)

V.P. MARLEY. Where was I? Oh, that's right. *(He kneels again.)* Sweetheart. I want to make you the happiest woman in the world.

SOPHIA. But –.

V.P. MARLEY. I know it's sudden. But I know in my heart that you love me and I love you.

(He reaches into his pocket. He can't find it.)

V.P. MARLEY. I think you'll like this…Where is it? It was here a minute ago. Must've left it in the Porsche.

SOPHIA. Left what?

(He heads for the door.)

V.P. MARLEY. Don't move. I'll be right back. Sit. Stay.

(He exits. The phone rings. **SOPHIA** *answers.)*

SOPHIA. *(on phone)*…Mom, he's going to propose…

*(***PHIL*** *comes out of hiding.)*

PHIL. You can't be serious. Sophia, he's a schmuck.

SOPHIA. *(on phone)* Mom, I got a funny feeling about this one. I'm not sure I love him.

PHIL. Exactly! Love is what it's all about.

SOPHIA. *(on phone)* Yes, I know, beggars can't be choosers but, Mom, I'm not so sure I'm a beggar yet.

PHIL. Trust me you're not.

SOPHIA. *(on phone)* …I know, I know, you're a better judge.…Yes, I know all my friends are married and have kids. Yes, even cousin Tundy…Twice? Really?

PHIL. Sophia, he's not right for you. He talks to you like you're a dog. Sit. Stay.

SOPHIA. *(on phone)* …Mom, I'm confused – I've never dated someone with a condo in Cancun…You're right. It's time I wake up and realize that all men are jerks, so I might as well marry a rich jerk. It totally makes sense. Can I call you back? I gotta think…and throw up.

*(***SOPHIA*** *hangs up and exits to the bathroom.)*

PHIL. *(to the audience)* I know what you're thinking. The ring. It's the Myth of Gyges. Plato's *Republic Book*

Two. ...Come on now we've all read Plato's *Republic*! You know the point where Glaucon defends the idea that if no one is watching, human beings will always pursue their own self-interest. Okay okay, for the Phys-ed majors out there, the Myth of Gyges for beginners. Gyges is a shepherd in the service of the king when there's this earthquake. His flock takes off but Gyges stays and is amazed to find a chasm has opened in the earth. Down below he finds a hollow horse. Inside a dead body wearing a golden ring. He takes the ring and tries it on. It fits. While playing with it, he twists it and instantly he becomes invisible. He twists it back and reappears! Thinking this is pretty cool, Gyges, goes to the royal court and, using his newfound powers, seduces the queen, kills the king and takes power – just as you would do. Oh come on, if you could become invisible, what would you do? Anything you could get away with.

(NORMAN knocks on the door.)

NORMAN. *(in a panic – through the door)* Hello? Hello? Sophia? It's Norm from work? Sophia? Has a messenger named Phil stopped by – ?

(NORMAN pokes his head in.)

NORMAN. Phil! I knew it! When you disappeared, I knew it!

PHIL. I've had an epiphany.

NORMAN. Does she know you're here?

PHIL. No.

NORMAN. Where is she?

PHIL. Bathroom.

NORMAN. Let's go.

PHIL. No wait. Don't you see, humans are only self-inter-ested. And so he'll marry his third trophy wife and she'll marry money. But love isn't part of the equation.

NORMAN. Is being fired part of the equation?

SOPHIA. *(from the bathroom)* Sweetheart, that you?

PHIL. No, it's just Norm and I.

NORMAN. *(panicked whispering)* What're you doing?!

PHIL. Proving a point. She can't hear me either.

NORMAN. Are you nuts?!

SOPHIA. *(from the bathroom)* You want nuts? There might be some in the kitchen.

PHIL. But she can hear you.

> *(The phone rings.* **NORMAN** *dives for cover behind the couch just as* **SOPHIA** *enters.)*

SOPHIA. *(on phone)* Hello? *(beat)* Very funny, Mom...How did I know it was you? Who else would call making a ticking sound? Yes, I know my biological clock is ticking...I'm hanging up...No you cannot stay with us in Cancun.

> *(She hangs up and runs back into the bathroom.* **NORMAN** *comes out of hiding.)*

NORMAN. Let's go!

PHIL. I'm staying.

NORMAN. But Marley'll be here any moment!

PHIL. It's okay, I can't be sure, but I don't think he can see me either.

NORMAN. You've lost it. You're as nutty as a fruitcake and you're fired! I mean it Phil, this is goodbye! Our friendship is over!

> *(***NORMAN** *starts for the door. Just as he gets there,* **V.P. MARLEY** *knocks.)*

V.P. MARLEY. *(calling through the door)* Sweetheart?

NORMAN. Hide me!

PHIL. Me first!

> *(***PHIL** *and* **NORMAN** *fight to get in the closet.)*

NORMAN. But I thought you said he couldn't see you!

PHIL. That's just a theory!

> *(***NORMAN** *shoves* **PHIL** *out of the way and climbs in the closet.* **PHIL** *tries to hide behind a plant but it's too small. He puts a lampshade on his head just as* **V.P. MARLEY** *enters with a ring box.)*

V.P. MARLEY. Sweetheart, I'm back.

(**SOPHIA** *enters.* **V.P. MARLEY** *looks directly at* **PHIL.**)

V.P. MARLEY. Who the hell is that?

SOPHIA. What's that, sweetheart?

V.P. MARLEY. Him.

PHIL. Look, Vice President Marley –

SOPHIA. Who?

V.P. MARLEY. That guy?

PHIL. I can explain –

V.P. MARLEY. An old boyfriend?

PHIL. Boyfriend?

SOPHIA. Oh that. That's not an old boyfriend. That's my brother.

(**SOPHIA** *walks right past* **PHIL** *and takes a photo of her brother off the wall.* **PHIL** *is relieved.*)

V.P. MARLEY. Didn't know you had a brother.

SOPHIA. Two. Twins.

V.P. MARLEY. Glad to hear it. One thing I hate is competition.

PHIL. Norm. I was right he can't see me either!

V.P. MARLEY. Sit. Where was I. Oh! I was on my knees wasn't I?

SOPHIA. Richard –.

(**V.P. MARLEY** *gets on his knees.*)

V.P. MARLEY. No no, stay. Good girl. As I was saying, I love you and –

SOPHIA. Richard –

V.P. MARLEY. No you don't have to say it, I already know, you love me.

SOPHIA. No. Maybe this isn't such a good idea.

PHIL. Did you hear that Norm? She's going to turn him down.

V.P. MARLEY. Oh God, here we go again.

SOPHIA. What?

V.P. MARLEY. Sophia, you're thinking.

SOPHIA. Yes, there are very important philosophical questions to answer. Like what is marriage? What is love?

PHIL. Do I exist?

V.P. MARLEY. Sophia, sweetheart, relax your mind.

SOPHIA. But –

V.P. MARLEY. Shhhhh. All you need to know is that I love you.

SOPHIA. What's love?

V.P. MARLEY. I don't know.

SOPHIA. If you can't define it, then how do you know you love me?

PHIL. Damn she's good.

V.P. MARLEY. Why can't you just accept the fact that I'm here, I have a ring. You'll live in comfort. You'll be happy.

SOPHIA & PHIL. But what's happiness?

V.P. MARLEY. Happiness is…is happiness!

SOPHIA. But according to different philosophical views it might be self-actualization – or just a lack of pain.

V.P. MARLEY. All right, fine. Happiness is a…a feeling. A feeling I get when I look in your eyes.

SOPHIA. My eyes make you happy?

V.P. MARLEY. Yes.

SOPHIA. Richard, there's something you need to know about me –.

(V.P. MARLEY opens the ring box revealing a spectacular diamond engagement ring.)

SOPHIA. *(taken by the shiny ring)* Oh my.

PHIL. Oh no. Sophia, you're not going to fall for that. It's just a ring. A trinket – *(seeing the ring)* More than my life's salary.

V.P. MARLEY. Sophia, sweetheart, perhaps spending your life questioning everything isn't so great. I mean sometimes you just need to let life come to you. So I'm asking you – from the bottom of my heart – Will you marry me?

PHIL. *(still taken by the ring)* I do.

SOPHIA. *(still taken by the ring)* I…

V.P. MARLEY. Three and a half karats with one karat insets.

SOPHIA. I…

V.P. MARLEY. All you have to do is say "yes" and I'll make you happy. I may not know what happiness is, I may not know a lot of things, but I'll make you happy.

SOPHIA. Everything's happening so fast. I'm confused.

V.P. MARLEY. What's confusing about this? I want to take you out of this horrible subterranean cave you call an apartment and have you live with me in a seventeen-room luxury condo with two Jacuzzis overlooking Central Park. What's confusing about that?

PHIL. You know he's got a point.

SOPHIA. Richard…I can't.

(The phone rings. SOPHIA unplugs it.)

SOPHIA. Richard, all my life I've wanted someone to say those words. When I was a kid, my girl friends and I would play "wedding proposal." We'd take rings from crackerjack boxes and stage spectacular proposals. One of us would play a knight in shining armor and would pretend to ride up on a horse and pop the question. Or we'd build a restaurant out of old boxes and folding chairs in the garage and we'd find a ring hidden in the dessert. But –

V.P. MARLEY. But what?

SOPHIA. I'm sorry.

*(**PHIL** does a little celebration dance. He's a really bad dancer.)*

PHIL. Score!

V.P. MARLEY. No woman has ever said that to me before.

SOPHIA. I want to say yes, but I can't until I answer certain philosophical questions.

V.P. MARLEY. What? It's not big enough?

SOPHIA. Size isn't important to me.

PHIL. This is the beginning of a beautiful relationship.

V.P. MARLEY. Then what?

SOPHIA. I think we need commonalities.

V.P. MARLEY. We have tons.

PHIL. Like what? Name one.

V.P. MARLEY. Ah…we both work in the same building. On the same floor. And we both like…coffee.

PHIL. She drinks green tea! I know that and you don't!

SOPHIA. Richard, I drink green tea.

V.P. MARLEY. Okay, hot drinks in general.

SOPHIA. If you could just come up with one thing, one little thing we have in common, I'd marry you in a millisecond. But we need something that we can share.

V.P. MARLEY. Fine. I'll just go home.

SOPHIA. I'm so sorry.

V.P. MARLEY. Seventeen rooms of nothing – nothing but my mother.

SOPHIA. …You live with your mother?

V.P. MARLEY. No. She's in the condo above me. She's always butting into my life. Calling me every five seconds.

SOPHIA. You're kidding.

PHIL. Oh no.

SOPHIA. My mother lives upstairs and calls me every five seconds.

V.P. MARLEY. Sometimes I think—.

V.P. MARLEY & SOPHIA. She's listening in.

(beat)

SOPHIA. *(holding out her ring finger)* I accept.

V.P. MARLEY & PHIL. What?

SOPHIA. I think we should share stock options.

PHIL. You can't be serious!

(V.P. MARLEY quickly slips the ring on her finger. With no depth perception, she has a little trouble getting it on.

She admires it.)

SOPHIA. It's beautiful.

(They kiss. It's great for him. Okay for her. **PHIL** *is grossed out.)*

PHIL. Ewwww.

V.P. MARLEY. Now that we are engaged, we have to be honest with each other. Tell me something you've never told another man.

SOPHIA. Like?

V.P. MARLEY. A secret.

SOPHIA. Okay…Many years ago my younger brother got this BB gun for Christmas – This is so hard to say,… Rich, I don't want you to hate me, but I have –.

V.P. MARLEY. A file that you took off my desk.

SOPHIA. A what?

V.P. MARLEY. Come on Sophia. I accidentally left a V.I.P. file on my desk during the merger meeting. You must've taken it.

SOPHIA. I don't know what you're talking about.

V.P. MARLEY. A file! With papers in it!

SOPHIA. Why is this file so important?

V.P. MARLEY. It just is!

SOPHIA. I don't know anything about –.

V.P. MARLEY. *(responding to earpiece)* Shut up!

SOPHIA. What?

V.P. MARLEY. *(on earphone)* Shut up! You have got to be kidding. No, She doesn't have it…Right…Right *(hangs up)* Look, sweetheart, gotta run. But before I leave, do me one favor. Look me in the eye and say it.

SOPHIA. Say what?

V.P. MARLEY. You didn't take the file.

SOPHIA. I didn't take the file.

V.P. MARLEY. What's wrong with your eye?

SOPHIA. …Allergies.

V.P. MARLEY. Gotta run.

(V.P. MARLEY heads for the door.)

SOPHIA. But –.

V.P. MARLEY. Can I have the ring back?

SOPHIA. What?

V.P. MARLEY. I should get it sized. Tell you what, tomorrow after everything settles we can go find a better one.

SOPHIA. But this is the one you proposed with.

V.P. MARLEY. You like it, huh?

SOPHIA. I love it!

V.P. MARLEY. Okay, but don't lose it. Oh, give me one more for the road.

(V.P. MARLEY kisses SOPHIA. While they kiss PHIL turns to the audience.)

PHIL. I know what you're thinking, she's kissing an asshole.

V.P. MARLEY. Be a good girl.

(V.P. MARLEY runs out. SOPHIA gazes at the ring.)

SOPHIA. Wow.

PHIL. Sophia. I don't want to say it but I've lost all respect for you. I'm thinking it but I'm not saying it.

(SOPHIA plugs in the phone – it rings immediately.)

SOPHIA. *(on phone)* Hi Mom...yes he did...yes, it's huge!

PHIL. I thought you said size doesn't matter.

SOPHIA. *(on phone)* Maybe I've been wrong. Maybe I've been wrong about a lot of things... Mom, I gotta go look at it in the mirror. I'll call you back.

(SOPHIA hangs up.)

SOPHIA. *(admiring the ring)* Wow.

(She runs into the bathroom.)

(NORMAN pops his head out of the closet.)

NORMAN. Gone?

PHIL. I can't believe it. She just changed. An intelligent thinking woman became a sack of blubber because of a ring. I mean you think you know someone. Perhaps the pre-Socratic philosophers were right – You can't really know anything. And if anything was knowable it couldn't be communicated from one person to another. Therefore, nothing really exists –.

(NORMAN punches PHIL in the stomach.)

PHIL. *(in pain)* Why?

(PHIL goes down.)

NORMAN. What about my fist? Is my fist knowable? Cause I think I just communicated the existence of my fist. Am I right?

PHIL. *(trying to draw air)* Your fist exists.

NORMAN. And if my fist exists then I must exist. Now that I exist, I'm going back to my crappy little office and try to save my crappy little job. And one other thing, you're fired. Don't bother coming back to the office. I'll pack up your stuff and leave it with security. And as for our friendship that too is over. I am not a wallflower!

(The phone rings.)

NORMAN. Crap. Hide me!

(NORMAN dives into the kitchenette just as SOPHIA enters wearing her eye patch. She puts the eye in its special box and answers the phone.)

SOPHIA. *(on the phone)* Hi Mom…Can I show it to you tomorrow?…So much has happened, I think I'll just take a shower, get into bed and watch CSPAN. Yes Mom, I won't blow it this time, I promise.

(She hangs up. NORMAN watches as she heads for the bathroom taking off her blouse – only this time she leaves the door open. We hear the sound of the shower being turned on.)

PHIL. Wow.

(NORMAN comes out of hiding.)

NORMAN. You are nuts! Nuts!

(NORMAN runs out.)

(Steam flows from the bathroom door.)

PHIL. *(to the audience)* I know what you're thinking. It all comes down to morals. Okay, let's start with the basics.

(SOPHIA's blouse flies out of the bathroom.)

PHIL. *(to the audience)* The Golden Rule: We should do to others what we would want others to do to us. Well, that goes without saying, I'd love it if Sophia took a shower with me and so I'm in fact treating her exactly as I would want her to treat me!

(SOPHIA's bra flies out of the bathroom and lands, hope-fully, on PHIL's head.)

PHIL. *(to the audience)* But what about Immanuel Kant's cat-egorical imperative: Treat people as an end, and never as a means to an end. But is taking a shower with a beautiful rational being who doesn't know you exist really treating her as a means? I mean cleanliness is next to godliness.

(SOPHIA's pantyhose fly out.)

PHIL. *(to the audience)* Or what about consequentialism: An action is morally right if the consequences of that action are more favorable than unfavorable. Once again I win. This is very favorable and no one suffers!

(SOPHIA's panties fly out.)

PHIL. *(to the audience)* Nietzsche wrote "Mankind's great-est labor so far has been to reach agreement about many things and to submit it to a law of agreement – regardless of whether these things are true or false." Which of course begs the question – would Nietzsche take a shower with a beautiful woman who doesn't know he exists? "A" Nietzsche was a man. "B" With-out question all men would choose to live out their fourteen-year-old fantasy. Therefore "C" Nietzsche was a fourteen-year-old boy! Am I better than Nietzsche?

Are you better than Nietzsche? No! And so I have no choice but to take a shower!

(**PHIL** *takes off his shirt.*)

PHIL. *(to the audience)* I am not a nice guy!

(As he enters the bathroom **PHIL** *sings – Steam flows. The lights fade.)*

End of Act One

ACT TWO

(The lights rise. The sofa-sleeper is now a bed. SOPHIA sleeps – nothing for a moment. Then PHIL pokes his head out from under the covers. His head is next to her feet.)

PHIL. *(to the audience)* I know what you're thinking, and you're right, I am the happiest man in the world. But just so you know – I couldn't go through with the shower. I know I know, the men out there are very disappointed with me. But it occurred to me that I'm not interested in a one-night stand – or one shower for that matter. And so I waited out here, like a perfect gentleman, a nice guy, until she was done, then I asked her out on our first date. She didn't say "no." I realize that's because she doesn't know I was asking her but I'm okay with that. It was a fantastic date. I dominated the conversation, talked only about myself – she didn't mind. Then we watched three PBS specials in a row: String Theory, Global Warming and Cajun Cooking with Bill Moyers. I even farted – she was okay with it. I asked her to go out dancing tonight. And guess what, she didn't say "no." Ayn Rand said, "To live, man must hold three things as the supreme and ruling values of his life: reason, purpose and self-esteem." I think Ayn would be pleased – I'm being very reasonable, I finally have a purpose and my self-esteem has never been higher.

(The phone rings. SOPHIA wakes up, turns on the lamp and answers. She takes off her sleeping mask to reveal her eye patch.)

SOPHIA. *(groggy)* Hello…What?…Mom it's too early –. Who?…Wait a sec. Let me find my glasses.

(**SOPHIA** *searches for her glasses on the nightstand.*)

PHIL. *(to the audience)* Why do we cohabitate: Love? Companionship? Propagation of the species? I'm convinced that men and women are supposed to be together but they're not supposed to *be* together.

SOPHIA. *(putting on her glasses)* Now I can hear you. Who's this?…Norm? It's five thirty in the morn – …What?… Okay, okay…I'll be right there. Give me five minutes.

(She hangs up and hurries to the bathroom.)

*(**PHIL** gets out of bed; he's fully dressed.)*

PHIL. *(to the audience)* Follow my logic – Every problem you've ever had in a relationship happened when the other person was present, am I right? The problem with relationships is that we are constantly bumping into each other. Guys, if you could shack up with a woman, yet avoid detection, wouldn't that be fantastic? Ladies, if you could cohabitate with a man, but not have the slightest inkling of his presence, wouldn't that be heaven?

*(The phone rings. Half dressed, **SOPHIA** runs in and answers.)*

SOPHIA. *(on phone)* Look, Norm, I said I'd be there –. Oh Mom…Yes, that was the phone. They called me in. Some sort of emergency at work…What?…No, no one stayed here last night…What do you mean you could hear a man singing in my shower?

PHIL. *(to the audience)* It's not what you think. After she went to bed I took a cold shower. Alone.

SOPHIA. *(on phone)* Mom, I assure you I was alone last night. …Completely and totally alone…You don't have to be so disappointed. Look, Mom, gotta run…Yes, tick-tock tick-tock.

*(**SOPHIA** hangs up and runs back to the bathroom.)*

PHIL. *(to the audience)* I understand that there is no physical or scientific reason for my being here yet not being here. Nietzsche, 1844–1900, said that science cannot be used to understand everything. He uses music as an example. We can scientifically count, calculate and formulate a melody but do such scientific estimations make for comprehension? So I don't try to comprehend what's happening, I'm just enjoying the music.

(Still dressing, **SOPHIA** *runs in and heads for the door.)*

PHIL. Don't forget your eye, dear.

SOPHIA. Oh, that's right.

*(***SOPHIA** *grabs her eye and runs back into the bathroom)*

PHIL. I think I'll just hang around today, drink beer, leave the toilet seat up and not do a darn thing. I hope you don't mind.

*(***SOPHIA** *runs in adjusting her eye.)*

PHIL. Didn't think you would.

(He throws her a kiss. She grabs her coat and heads for the door. But with no depth perception, she has to grope for the door handle. She exits.)

PHIL. *(singing)* You make me feel like dancing!

(Whistling a happy tune, **PHIL** *goes through her CD collection.)*

PHIL. Let's see what we've got. "The very best of the Bee Gees – Volume One." And "Volume Two" wow. "The Bee Gees, 1963-1966: The Birth of Brilliance." Very cool.

(He turns on the stereo and flips in the CD. Disco music blares. He dances – He can't dance. After a few missteps he turns the music down.)

PHIL. *(to the audience)* Heard a joke the other day. René Descartes walks into a bar and the bartender says, "Hey René, how about a beer?" And René says, "I think not." And disappears. Get it? He disappears.

(He turns the music back up, grabs **SOPHIA**'s *eye patch, puts it on and dances.)*

(In a panic, **NORMAN** *comes to the door and knocks.)*

NORMAN. Phil? Phil?!

*(***PHIL** *dances over to the door. Checks the peep hole and unlocks.* **NORMAN** *enters.* **PHIL** *continues to dance.)*

NORMAN. What are you doing? Dancing?

*(***NORMAN** *flips off the music.)*

NORMAN. Is she gone?

PHIL. *(imitating a pirate)* Aye! – She be called into work.

NORMAN. I know, that was me! Let's get out of here because I found out that – *(seeing the open bed)* You didn't. You did! You spent the night!

PHIL. Aye.

NORMAN. Without her knowledge?

PHIL. Aye.

NORMAN. Would you stop doing that!

PHIL. Aye aye, captain.

*(***NORMAN** *pulls off the eye patch.)*

NORMAN. Phil, I don't know what's going on here, but you gotta come with me now.

PHIL. I thought our friendship was over. If I remember correctly someone punched someone else in the stomach.

NORMAN. Sorry, I over reacted – you're rehired, but you gotta come with me. Something's come up concerning the merger!

PHIL. No way. Sophia and I are in love.

NORMAN. How can you be in love – she doesn't know you exist!

PHIL. I admit it; it's not an ideal love. But according to Plato that's not possible anyway. All we can do is imitate the eternal truths that are the source of reality. So this is a very good imitation of love, but not the real thing. I'm okay with that.

NORMAN. But it's sick.

PHIL. No, It's an imitation of the idea "sick," but not really sick –

NORMAN. Get your coat and shoes.

PHIL. I've discovered that you're right, invisibility is wonderful!

*(***NORMAN*** *searches for* ***PHIL****'s coat, socks, and shoes.)*

NORMAN. I'm not invisible.

PHIL. Sure you are. You just hide in plain sight.

NORMAN. Where are your shoes?

PHIL. I mean if you think about it, the spotlight sucks. Let your presence be known and people start expecting things. But stay under the radar and you can wander through the mass of humanity without disturbing anything. This is what you do.

NORMAN. I do not. I exist. Where are your socks?

PHIL. If anyone doesn't even register a blip, it's you.

NORMAN. Coming from an invisible pervert, that really hurts.

PHIL. I meant it as a compliment. At work you give no clue of your presence. Lot's of people don't – Some are just fuzzy, others overlooked, but you Norm, you're the master at the art of invisibility. You don't walk too fast or too slow. Your clothes aren't bland but you don't stand out. Because you know that if you're noticed you can be assessed, judged and held accountable.

NORMAN. Put your shoes on.

PHIL. You can't be fired cause no one knows what you do and Sophia can't break up with me cause she doesn't know I'm dating her – we are the heroes of the twenty-first century! We play it safe!

NORMAN. Phil, I've been up all night working on the Mead Report – it's not good. Then Marley storms into my office and orders me to call Sophia in. Saw my chance. I knew she'd be out so I saved your butt. That's not playing it safe.

PHIL. I'm sorry to hear that, cause I'll never take a chance again.

NORMAN. Phil, Sophia's going to marry Marley. What're you going to do then?

PHIL. Hadn't thought that far ahead yet.

NORMAN. This is why you should never hire philosophy majors – they have no perception of reality!

PHIL. Oh my god! That's it! The problem is perception! Descartes was right, that which is seen with the eye can only be grasped with the faculty of judgment. Follow my logic.

NORMAN. Please don't make me follow your logic.

PHIL. If you grew up in a society where there were no… let's say…chairs for example.

NORMAN. He's talking about chairs.

PHIL. Everyone either stood or laid down but no one ever thought of sitting. What would happen the first time you saw a chair?

NORMAN. I don't know I might use it to crack my former best friend's head open?

PHIL. No, you wouldn't know what it was. As far as you were concerned that chair would be an object with no purpose, and so you wouldn't perceive it as a chair! Immanuel Kant, 1724 – 1804, was right. The world that we perceive, imagine, and interpret can only be passed through the human mind's categories of understanding. Or as John Locke, 1632 – 1704, said – ,

NORMAN. Would you stop it with the dates!

PHIL. "Man's knowledge can't go beyond his experience." Don't you see?

NORMAN. See what?

PHIL. There's no category marked chair!

NORMAN. So?!

PHIL. I'm the chair!

NORMAN. Okay, you're a chair, let's go.

PHIL. Sophia has never with her mind's eye or through cultural or social interaction met or pictured a nice guy and so she cannot perceive one. We must make her understand that such a chair exists!

NORMAN. A chair like you.

PHIL. Yes! A chair like me!

NORMAN. But what about Vice President Marley – why can't he see you?

PHIL. Oh him. He's just an asshole.

(A knock at the door.)

V.P. MARLEY. *(calling through the door)* Sweetheart?

NORMAN. Crap. It's the asshole. Hide!

PHIL. Closet!

(PHIL opens the closet door. NORMAN jumps inside just as V.P. MARLEY enters.)

V.P. MARLEY. Sweetheart, are you here. Honey-bun?

(V.P. MARLEY walks right past PHIL and looks in the bathroom. PHIL stands in plain sight.)

PHIL. Why are you here?

V.P. MARLEY. Sweet-things?

(V.P. MARLEY begins looking through her drawers.)

PHIL. You told Norman to call her into work so you could break in. But why?

(V.P. MARLEY sees a file box and begins going through it.)

PHIL. *(to the audience)* I know what you're thinking. Relativism – am I right? The idea that right and wrong vary considerably from place to place and time to time; therefore, there are no universally valid ethical standards –I'm mean, I'm sure that he can justify this. I'm sure that in his own mind breaking into his fiancée's apartment is ethical. But is it moral?

(V.P. MARLEY doesn't see SOPHIA enter. They jump when they see each other.)

SOPHIA & V.P. MARLEY. Ahhhh!

PHIL. Okay, things are going to get interesting.

SOPHIA. Richard!

V.P. MARLEY. Sophia!

SOPHIA. What are you doing?

V.P. MARLEY. I was trying to find your…

SOPHIA. Yes?

V.P. MARLEY. …Engagement ring!

SOPHIA. My what?

V.P. MARLEY. I noticed that it was a little loose and was going to have it sized.

SOPHIA. At 6 o'clock in the morning?

V.P. MARLEY. I know a 24-hour jewelry store?

SOPHIA. Then how come you're going through my files?

V.P. MARLEY. I don't know where a woman would keep a ring.

SOPHIA. Perhaps in my jewelry box. Or on my finger.

V.P. MARLEY. Oh, you're wearing it of course. Sometimes men can be such fools.

PHIL. You're not going to buy that Sophia.

SOPHIA. You expect me to buy that?

V.P. MARLEY. Yes – Because it's the truth.

PHIL. *(knocking on the closet door)* Hey Norman, do you believe this guy?

SOPHIA. Richard…sometimes your behavior confuses me.

V.P. MARLEY. I know I'm a fool.

SOPHIA. Trust is important in a relationship. If you wanted the ring just ask.

V.P. MARLEY. I came by to pick you up. Realized you had already left, remembered the ring, the door was open so I let myself in.

SOPHIA. No. I locked my door.

V.P. MARLEY. It was open when I got here. Look, next time I'll think before I do something so stupid. The fact that you caught me has really made me think.

SOPHIA. You're worried about detection?

V.P. MARLEY. Aren't we all?

SOPHIA. Oh my god, Richard, do you realize what you're saying?

V.P. MARLEY. Not always.

SOPHIA. It's Gyges.

PHIL. Bingo!

V.P. MARLEY. Who?

SOPHIA. The myth of Gyges.

V.P. MARLEY. Right. Of course. That's the one with the Hobbits right?

SOPHIA. It's the idea that moral behavior in human beings can only be motivated by a fear of detection and punishment. Richard, we can't have a relationship based on that.

PHIL. You tell'em sweetheart.

V.P. MARLEY. When you're right, you're right. I wasn't thinking. Look, Sophia, sweetheart, I was sitting up at my office just now, pulling an all-nighter, and all I could think is, damn I miss her. So I came up with this silly plot to call you in.

PHIL. He's lying.

V.P. MARLEY. Sweetheart, do you know what I love about you?

SOPHIA. I know, my eyes.

V.P. MARLEY. No, it's your brains that really turn me on.

SOPHIA. Really?

V.P. MARLEY. Brains first, intellect second – your eyes are a distant third. Maybe even fourth.

PHIL. Oh my god, you're not going to fall for that?

SOPHIA. Well, all right. But we have an agreement? We're not going to lie to each other anymore?

V.P. MARLEY. Never ever again. My lying days are over.

(They kiss.)

PHIL. *(to the audience)* I'm so ashamed of being a man right now.

SOPHIA. Let me get something. I'll be right back.

(She nonchalantly grabs her falsies and exits to the bathroom.)

PHIL. In the name of all wonderful, decent, caring men of the world, I have a message.

(PHIL *gives* V.P. MARLEY *the finger – about six inches from his face.* V.P. MARLEY *doesn't see this of course, checks to make sure the coast is clear and resumes his search.*)

SOPHIA. *(from the bathroom)* Oh, sweetheart, it's cold, get me a heavier jacket will you. It's in the closet.

V.P. MARLEY. The closet. Of course.

(*He heads for the closet.*)

PHIL. Norm, he's coming!

(V.P. MARLEY *searching the closet.*)

V.P. MARLEY. *(from the bathroom)* Which coat, the blue or green one?

SOPHIA. The red one in back.

PHIL. Don't worry, Norm, maybe he can't see you either.

(V.P. MARLEY *feels around for a moment.*)

V.P. MARLEY. What's this?

PHIL. Or I might be wrong about that.

(V.P. MARLEY *pulls* NORMAN *out of the closet by the neck.*)

NORMAN. Hello sir.

V.P. MARLEY. It's you…

NORMAN. Yes. Norman, sir.

V.P. MARLEY. Norman?

NORMAN. Yes, sir, I work for you sir and I can explain.

V.P. MARLEY. Explain what?

NORMAN. What I'm doing in Sophia's closet.

V.P. MARLEY. No need.

(*Just as* SOPHIA *enters,* V.P. MARLEY *punches* NORMAN *in the stomach.* PHIL *runs to* NORMAN*'s aid.*)

SOPHIA. What the – ?

V.P. MARLEY. *(to* **SOPHIA***)* You wanna talk about honesty! Wanna give me another little lecture about morals!

SOPHIA. Norm, what are you – ?

V.P. MARLEY. All this crap about philosophy and ethics, but when it comes right down to it, you're the one with a man hiding in the closet.

SOPHIA. Richard, I swear I know nothing about this – !

V.P. MARLEY. Sitting around trying to answer philosophical questions that have no answer while your lover hides in the closet!

SOPHIA. He's not my lover!

V.P. MARLEY. And of all things an accountant – oh the shame, Sophia, the shame.

SOPHIA. I swear he's not my lover!

V.P. MARLEY. Then why is he hiding?

SOPHIA. I don't know! Let's ask him! Norman, why are you hiding in my closet!

*(*V.P. MARLEY *picks* NORMAN *up by his collar.)*

V.P. MARLEY. I want answers.

NORMAN. Well sir. I came over to…ah…ah…

V.P. MARLEY. You'd better start talking!

PHIL. Tell'em you came over to pick her up. Noticed the door was open. Heard someone coming, panicked and hid.

V.P. MARLEY. If I don't get an answer you are so fired.

PHIL. Tell him you were trying to find the missing file! Say anything just stay under the radar.

V.P. MARLEY. I'm waiting!

NORMAN. …I'm not a wallflower.

V.P. MARLEY. A what?

PHIL. Norm, don't do this. You got a wife and kids –.

NORMAN. Shut up!

V.P. MARLEY. Did you just tell me to shut up?

NORMAN. No, I was talking to Phil.

SOPHIA. Who's Phil?

NORMAN. My assistant.

V.P. MARLEY. There's another man hiding in the closet? *(to* **SOPHIA***)* You sick, sick woman.

NORMAN. I'm just saying that this all started because of Phil – This isn't easy. You see, sometimes, there are things that aren't visible. I mean, sometimes we don't see things that are going on right under our noses. You must understand sir, I go to work everyday and I deal with numbers. I look at them so much that sometimes I don't see numbers anymore – I see only lines and curves.

V.P. MARLEY. Just tell me why you're hiding in the closet!

NORMAN. It's been right in front of my nose for months yet I never saw it. But now I have to tell you...

V.P. MARLEY. Tell me what?!

NORMAN. The books are cooked.

SOPHIA. What books?

NORMAN. The Mead deal is a sham. There are two sets of books. It's all part of a plan to inflate revenues.

V.P. MARLEY. Are you calling me a crook?

NORMAN. No, sir...Well, yes, sir –.

*(*V.P. MARLEY *rears back to punch* NORMAN.*)*

SOPHIA. Richard, stop!

V.P. MARLEY. *(to* NORMAN*)* What the hell do you know about business, you're nothing but a low level bean counter!

(The phone rings. SOPHIA *answers)*

SOPHIA. *(on the phone)* Mom! Later!

(She hangs up.)

V.P. MARLEY. My father and I worked all our lives to make this company! How dare you suggest that my father is crooked?

NORMAN. Not your father, sir, just you. Your father is just senile.

(V.P. MARLEY punches NORMAN. SOPHIA screams.)

V.P. MARLEY. And if the day should ever come that we do find any accounting irregularities I'll make sure that one peon accountant is to blame. Sophia, let's get out of here.

(V.P. MARLEY heads for the door. SOPHIA delays.)

V.P. MARLEY. Sophia, come! Now!

SOPHIA. Norm, I'm sorry.

V.P. MARLEY. Sophia! Come!

(V.P. MARLEY hustles SOPHIA out.)

PHIL. Norm, what were you thinking, you broke the first rule of invisibility.

NORMAN. *(in pain)* I'm not a wallflower.

PHIL. You're also no longer employed.

NORMAN. I told the truth. The books are cooked.

PHIL. Of course they are.

NORMAN. You knew?

PHIL. It's as plain as the nose on your face! I've known for a year. I thought you knew.

NORMAN. I'm so blind. I just figured it out this morning. That's why I came over here –.

(SOPHIA runs back in.)

SOPHIA. Answer me one question.

PHIL. Sophia –.

SOPHIA. Are you the one who has been writing the letters?

NORMAN. What letters?

SOPHIA. The sweet and low letters?

PHIL. Oh my god, she got my love letters!

NORMAN. No. It wasn't me. It was Phil.

SOPHIA. Phil? Who's Phil?

NORMAN. My assistant – the man who's in love with you.

SOPHIA. And he's living in my closet with you?

NORMAN. No, you can't see him.

SOPHIA. Why not?

NORMAN. Because you don't know what a chair is.

V.P. MARLEY. *(offstage)* Sophia? Sophia!

(**V.P. MARLEY** *enters.*)

V.P. MARLEY. What the hell is the problem?

SOPHIA. I, ah…Forgot my…scarf.

V.P. MARLEY. Fetch it and let's go.

SOPHIA. Richard –.

(**SOPHIA** *delays.*)

V.P. MARLEY. What is it now?

SOPHIA. That file…the file you thought I took home with me?

V.P. MARLEY. What's this?

SOPHIA. Yesterday you thought I'd taken something from your desk.

V.P. MARLEY. They were just papers. Numbers. Graphs. Nothing important.

SOPHIA. So unimportant you came over and proposed marriage? So unimportant you broke into my apartment.

V.P. MARLEY. Look, sweetheart, a relationship is based on trust. If you don't trust me then we don't have a relationship.

SOPHIA. No we don't, do we?

V.P. MARLEY. You're breaking it off? Over some trivial files? They were nothing. Earnings reports from the Atlanta office. It's nothing. Let's go.

(**SOPHIA** *doesn't move.*)

SOPHIA. I need to check on my mother.

V.P. MARLEY. Who?

SOPHIA. My mother. Upstairs.

V.P. MARLEY. Fine. But if you're not in the car in five minutes it's over. Do we understand each other? I'll wait five minutes for any woman but that's all. Give me the ring.

SOPHIA. What?

V.P. MARLEY. The ring. Give.

SOPHIA. But –.

V.P. MARLEY. Give!

(**SOPHIA** *gives him the engagement ring.*)

V.P. MARLEY. See this? This isn't a ring. This is the future. And it's waiting down in the car. Five minutes. *(to* **NORMAN***)* You're a dead man.

*(***V.P. MARLEY** *exits.)*

NORMAN. I'm so sorry.

(beat)

SOPHIA. …I had a dream last night. I met a man. Unlike most men he didn't take advantage of the situation; instead he just told me that he loved me.

PHIL. That was me!

SOPHIA. And then he gently played with my hair…but he didn't try anything. It was refreshing. He just held me and let me know that I was safe.

PHIL. Tell her it was me!

NORMAN. Sophia –

SOPHIA. But I felt that no matter what happened, I'd never have to prove myself to him.

PHIL. Tell her; tell her that I'm here.

NORMAN. Sophia, it wasn't a dream –.

SOPHIA. And then I kissed him and I let a soft sigh escape to let him know that I now knew what perfection is. And then my dream flashed forward. It was graduation day. And our kids were over – all of them philosophy majors. And they told us that they'd all found jobs with full benefits. And then this man, my husband, began to disco dance to the Bee Gees. Only he couldn't dance. He was the worst dancer the world has ever known.

PHIL. Wait. Maybe it wasn't me. I can dance.

SOPHIA. In my dream, this man told me his name was… Phil.

PHIL. I'm Phil!

SOPHIA. Does such a man exist?

NORMAN. You're looking at him.

SOPHIA. Norm, that's very nice, but you're married.

NORMAN. No, not me. But you're looking at him – or through him. Sophia, I know what I'm about to say doesn't make a lick of sense. But he's here.

SOPHIA. Who's here?

NORMAN. Phil. You just can't see him.

SOPHIA. Perhaps it would be best if you left.

NORMAN. Wait, Sophia, something happened to me this morning also. I was working in my office, like I do every morning, when suddenly I noticed that my waste paper basket was empty. It had been overflowing just a moment before, but now it was empty. Isn't that strange I thought. Then I went into the hall and there I found…Angelina.

SOPHIA. Angelina?

NORMAN. The tenth floor cleaning woman. I asked her if she'd just emptied my trash. And she said yes. I asked her if she did this every morning. She said, every morning for the last three years. Isn't that amazing?

SOPHIA. Sure.

NORMAN. …Don't you see? For three years now Angelina has been coming into my office and I've never talked to her. Even said, "Hello." I mean, I was aware that my trash was being emptied, but I was never aware of her existence – does that make sense?

SOPHIA. No.

NORMAN. Just then it occurred to me that this happens all the time. Even two people walking hand in hand, on the same path, aren't necessarily aware of the other person's existence. Maybe, Sophia, just maybe if you open your eye you'll see someone is walking with you.

PHIL. That was beautiful, man.

NORMAN. Thanks.

SOPHIA. What did you just say?

PHIL. Huh?

SOPHIA. You said if I open my what?

NORMAN. Eyes.

SOPHIA. No, you said "eye" not "eyes."

NORMAN & PHIL. Oh crap.

SOPHIA. You know?

NORMAN. Yes. And so does Phil. It's no big deal.

SOPHIA. Get out! Both of you get out!

NORMAN. Look, Sophia. Practically everyone in the office knows.

SOPHIA. Everyone?

PHIL. Except Marley.

NORMAN. Everyone except the man you're supposedly going to marry. The man you're going to spend the rest of your life with.

(The phone rings.)

SOPHIA. *(on the phone)* …Yes Mom, I know there's a Porsche idling out front…yes, I know what a Porsche is…yes, Tick Tock Tick Tock!

(She hangs up. Beat.)

SOPHIA. Norman, it's been a pleasure working with you. Being Richard's secretary I'll arrange for a glowing letter of recommendation, signed by Mr. Marley's auto signer, to be waiting for you today when you clean out your desk. But, I'm sorry; I have a life waiting for me.

(She heads for the door.)

PHIL. Tell her I can prove I exist.

NORMAN. He can prove he exists.

SOPHIA. How can anyone prove they exist?

PHIL. I think therefore I exist.

NORMAN. He thinks therefore he –.

SOPHIA. Sorry Norm, that's not good enough. *(She stops at the door.)* I don't know why we're here. Or what our purpose is. But I do know that invisible-Phil is no use to me. Norm, take as long as you need. When you're done, turn off the lights and lock the door –.

(She turns to leave.)

PHIL. Lights! That's it!

NORMAN. Wait! I think he's got something.

PHIL. It's been right in front of us all along.

NORMAN. What has?

PHIL. Lights. And shadows.

NORMAN. So?

PHIL. Tell her that if she tries one thing, one little experiment, we'll leave her alone forever if it doesn't work.

NORMAN. Phil says that if you try one experiment and it doesn't work, he'll leave forever.

SOPHIA. What does he want?

PHIL. Plato's *Republic* Book Seven.

NORMAN. Plato's *Republic* Book Seven.

SOPHIA. I know it.

PHIL. Socrates is talking to a young follower named Glaucon.

NORMAN. Socrates is talking to Glaucon.

PHIL. What does Socrates say?

NORMAN. What does he say?

SOPHIA. Well…Socrates says that most people live in a world of relative ignorance. We're comfortable with our ignorance, because it's all we know.

PHIL. More.

NORMAN. Go on.

SOPHIA. Some are lucky enough to see beyond their ignorance.

PHIL. How does he make his point?

NORMAN. How does he make this point?

SOPHIA. Plato's Allegory of the Cave.

PHIL. Exactly. That's it! Problem solved!

NORMAN. Wait! For the non-philosophy majors in the room, what's Plato's Allegory of the Cave?

SOPHIA. Plato's cave analogy claims that we are all prisoners in a cave not seeing reality, but only a shadowy representation of it. Imagine human beings living in an underground den.

PHIL. Like this apartment.

SOPHIA. Our legs and necks chained so that we cannot move. We can only see a bare wall before us.

PHIL. Turn on that light. Point it towards the wall.

*(**NORMAN** turns on the reading lamp and points it at the bare wall.)*

SOPHIA. Above and behind us a fire is blazing so that all the prisoners see are shadows...as in a movie theatre, they don't see reality only a shadowy representation.

PHIL. Dim the lights.

*(**NORMAN** dims the lights. The reading lamp now makes a spotlight on the bare wall.)*

SOPHIA. The prisoners would never know that they are not seeing reality. We'd never be aware of the limits of their perspective. Plato believed that there are invisible truths underlying the apparent surface of things, which only the most enlightened can grasp.

PHIL. Perfect. Tell her that if this works she might be enlightened and freaked out a bit.

NORMAN. If this works it might freak us both out a bit.

PHIL. Here goes.

NORMAN. Watch.

*(Slowly **PHIL** puts his finger into the light. Its shadow appears on the wall.)*

NORMAN. Do you see that?

SOPHIA. *(dumbfounded)* Oh my.

*(**PHIL** now puts his entire hand into the light. Its shadow appears on the wall. He waves.)*

PHIL. Hello.

(**PHIL** *slowly steps into the light. The shadow of his whole body appears on the wall.*)

PHIL. I'm Phil...I'm the nice guy you're always overlooking.

SOPHIA. Oh...I'm Sophia.

NORMAN. Now do you believe me!

SOPHIA. I'm a little freaked out right now.

PHIL. Me too. I mean when this first happened. It was really strange, I didn't believe it myself, but now that I've lived with you for a while –.

SOPHIA. A while?

PHIL. Well, one night.

SOPHIA. You stayed here last night?

PHIL. Hypothetically, yes.

SOPHIA. Where did you hypothetically sleep?

PHIL. Ah...In your bed. But just like in your dream, I didn't try anything.

SOPHIA. So it was you my mother heard singing in my shower?

PHIL. ...Yes.

SOPHIA. You slept in my bed and used my shower.

PHIL. But you must understand, I was in a different reality.

SOPHIA. But what is reality?

PHIL. Reality depends on your perception.

SOPHIA. Then you would disagree with George Berkeley 1685 – 1753 who said, "To be is to be perceived –."

PHIL. I certainly don't want to detract from his argument but in my case I was and yet was not perceived and yet I did exist.

SOPHIA. How do you know you exist?

PHIL. "Cogito ergo sum." "I think therefore I exist."

SOPHIA. And what were you thinking when you used my shower and slept in my bed?

PHIL. I guess…

SOPHIA. Yes?

PHIL. I wasn't thinking.

SOPHIA. I rest my case.

PHIL. Have you seen the movie *The Matrix?*

SOPHIA. I own the trilogy –.

NORMAN. I hate to interrupt. But I have a feeling that this could go on for a while. The important thing is he's sorry.

SOPHIA. Okay. Can I ask you what you want?

PHIL. Ah…Nothing really. Just for you to acknowledge my existence?

SOPHIA. Okay. You exist.

PHIL. What do you want?

SOPHIA. …I don't know.

PHIL. Then why are you marrying Marley?

SOPHIA. I want to be happy.

PHIL. Aristotle pointed out that we pursue money, fame, power and material possessions because we believe these things will bring us happiness. But nobody seeks happiness in the belief that it'll bring them some higher benefit. So, with no higher benefit in mind, I just want to say…I love you.

SOPHIA. …Phil?

PHIL. Yes?

SOPHIA. This all makes sense.

PHIL. It does?

SOPHIA. There's just one small problem.

PHIL. What?

SOPHIA. …You're a nice guy.

PHIL. Yes! Yes, I am a nice guy!

SOPHIA. I don't date nice guys.

(beat)

(On the second empty wall beside **PHIL***'s shadow appears a new shadow – no person, just a shadow – It's the silhouette of a woman on crutches.)*

WOMAN'S SHADOW. *(Southern accent)* Hello? Hello? Phil? Phil, there you are!

PHIL. Oh my god!

SOPHIA. Who are you?

WOMAN'S SHADOW. It's Marybeth from accounts receivable. I've been following you around for days. I just want to say that I'm madly in love with you. So, why won't you acknowledge my existence!

*(**PHIL**, **NORMAN**, and **SOPHIA** look at each other and scream.)*

(blackout)

(The lights fade up on **PHIL** *in his office cubicle.)*

PHIL. *(to the audience)* I know what you're thinking. What's a soul? Aristotle said a soul was the "first principle of living things." Whether the soul is immortal or dies with the body doesn't really matter. Nor does it matter if we're dreaming or stuck in reality. All that's important is that souls exist. Yet, so many go unrecognized… for nothing exists except what a particular soul perceives – It's all relative. And that's the problem with humankind…we just haven't yet learned to get along with our relatives. *(beat)* Perhaps it's nothing more than a fleeting moment in a haphazard nebula that in the end utterly disappears. But it's my fleeting moment and I do have a soul and so I choose to seek out those fitful moments of happiness that are available. I now add Phil-from-accounting's addendum to Descartes' philosophical insight…I have loved therefore I exist.

*(**NORMAN** enters with a box containing his office belongings.)*

NORMAN. Hey buddy.

PHIL. I guess this is it. What can I say…sorry.

NORMAN. Don't be.

PHIL. If it hadn't been for my crazy antics, you'd still have a job.

NORMAN. And I'd still be unhappy. Do you know what made me unhappy?

PHIL. Working here?

NORMAN. Exactly.

(A squeak of speakers is heard. Disco music cuts in and out.)

V.P. MARLEY'S VOICE. *(over loud speakers)* Testing one two three. Testing one two three.

NORMAN. What's that?

PHIL. Marley's organized a big office party. The Mead merger went through this morning.

NORMAN. Then I should depart. Sorry things didn't work out with Sophia.

PHIL. Me too.

NORMAN. I heard she broke it off – the engagement.

PHIL. Good for her.

NORMAN. You're not going to...

PHIL. No, I've learned my lesson.

NORMAN. Don't worry, you'll find someone. Someday when you least expect it, you'll look up and see a face and it'll be the right face. And what's better, that face will see you.

MARLEY'S VOICE. *(from off stage speakers)* Hello, testing one two three. Testing. Is this working?...Good. What's our motto?

OFF STAGE OFFICE STAFF. Accountability and rock-solid ethical standards give us our competitive edge!

(Cheers and applause from the off stage office staff.)

NORMAN. By the way, I found out who took that file from Marley's desk. It was Angelina.

PHIL. The cleaning woman?

NORMAN. We're having lunch today. And then we're head-ing over to The New York Times. I think we have a story about a fraudulent merger they'll find most interesting – and the evidence to back it up.

MARLEY'S VOICE. *(from offstage speakers)* Are you ready to party?

(Cheers from the offstage office staff.)

MARLEY'S VOICE. *(from offstage speakers)* I can't hear you! Are you ready to party?!

(Louder cheers. A party can be heard.)

NORMAN. Strange isn't it? They're all in there partying and laughing and having a good old time, unaware that tomorrow will bring nothing but pink slips and painful disappointment.

PHIL. That's why we need philosophy. Schopenhauer – 1788-1860 – said, "philosophy turns our pain into knowledge."

NORMAN. …Seeya kid.

> *(**PHIL** and **NORMAN** shake. **NORMAN** exits. **SOPHIA** enters the break room with a tray of coffee. Her cellphone is tucked between her ear and her shoulder.)*

SOPHIA. *(on cell phone)* Mom…I can't talk right now. Cause I'm at work. Look Mom, my decision is final…Cause I gotta find a place of my own. Mom – No Mom, I'm quitting. I gave notice this morning – Mom, something happened last night and it got me thinking. I'm tired of dating jerks. Maybe it's time I start thinking outside the box –.

*(**SOPHIA** accidentally knocks over a coffee.)*

SOPHIA. Oh darn. *(on cell phone)* I'll have to call you back.

(She goes for the paper towels, but the roll is empty.)

PHIL. *(to the audience)* I know what you're thinking. Why aren't I helping her? It's simple; I've learned my lesson. Some women will never learn that nice guys exist. And they'll continue to date jerks – men who treat them poorly, men who cheat. There's nothing that can be done about it –

SOPHIA. *(to* **PHIL***)* Excuse me.

PHIL. *(to the audience)* Perception can be difficult. And some of us will go through life unaware of all life has to offer. We see only those things we want to see. Hear only those things we want to hear.

SOPHIA. *(to* **PHIL***)* Excuse me.

PHIL. *(to the audience)* But a few of us will set out to see those things we have not seen and hear things we have not heard.

SOPHIA. *(to* **PHIL***)* Excuse me, sir!

PHIL. …Are you talking to me?

SOPHIA. Yes. I could really use some paper towels.

PHIL. Sure.

*(***PHIL*** grabs the paper towels from beside his seat, runs over and helps her.)*

SOPHIA. Hey, thanks.

PHIL. …You're welcome. My pleasure.

SOPHIA. By the way, I'm Sophia.

(She offers her hand.)

PHIL. I'm…

SOPHIA. Yes?

PHIL. I'm…Philip.

SOPHIA. Oh. It's nice to meet you Philip.

(They shake.)

(While they hold hands the speakers squeak. Then loud 1980's disco music blares from the office party next door.)

*(***PHIL*** can't help himself. He begins to dance. **SOPHIA** watches as he does every bad disco move known. He puts a hand out for her to join him. She does. She can't dance either.)*

(A starry disco ball lowers. They disco dance. Then, as **PHIL** *strikes a triumphant John Travolta/*Saturday Night Fever *pose…)*

(blackout)

The End

PROP LIST

Bouquet of flowers
Box containing Norman's office belongings
Cell Phone
Cell phone (Hands-free ear type)
Coffee
Coffee cups
Diamond engagement ring
Eye patch
Falsies
Framed photo of Sophia's brother
Glass eye
Green tea
Love letters
Opera glasses
Paper towels
Papers & files
Ring box
Tray
Wallet

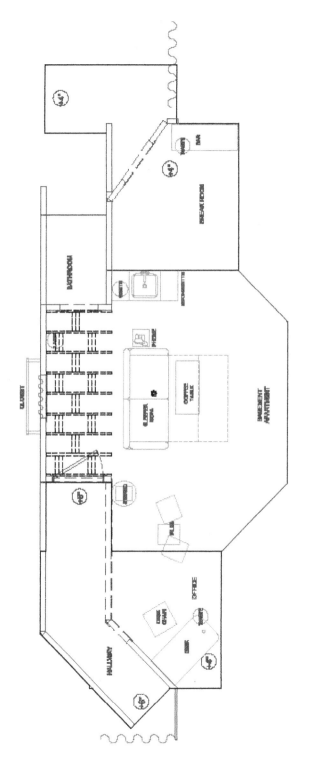

OTHER TITLES AVAILABLE FROM SAMUEL FRENCH

KOSHER LUTHERANS

William Missouri Downs

Comedy

2m, 3f

Unit Set

Kosher Lutherans centers on Hanna and Franklyn, the seemingly perfect couple who desperately want to have a child of their own, but are unable to do so. As the couple begins to wonder if they'll ever become parents, they have a chance encounter with a God-fearing pregnant girl from Iowa who offers to let the couple adopt her out-of-wedlock baby.

Just before the adoption papers are signed, Hanna and Franklyn discover the girl is unaware that they are Jewish. Knowing the revelation could throw a ratchet into the whole works, the couple poses as Lutherans to appeal to the girl's apparent Midwestern sensibilities. But how far are they willing to go to have a family?

OTHER TITLES AVAILABLE FROM SAMUEL FRENCH

COMEDY OF TERRORS

John Goodrum

Comedy/Farce

1m, 1f

Unit set

Jo Smith arrives at her local theatre for an audition with the director Vyvian Jones, but it transpires that she has actually been invited there by Beverley, Vyvian's twin brother, who wants her to impersonate her own twin sister Fiona in order to squelch the rumor that Beverley has slept with Fiona. (He has, but doesn't want Vyvian to tell his fiance Cheryl.) Jo reluctantly accepts this unusual acting job and pretends to be Fiona for Vyvian. But then the real Fiona arrives and thinks Vyvian is Beverley and then Vyvian, who is a member of the local Sons of Satan Association, takes Jo captive to use as a human sacrifice and then - Only the intervention of a policeman, Janet Jones (Beverley's and Vyvian's identical younger brother) can save the day as matters get more than a little confusing - One actor and one actress play all the Joneses and Smiths respectively in this fast-moving madcap comedy of multiple mistaken identity.